To my son Max, for the use of his tree – J. E.

For Humphrey – V. C.

Text copyright © 2001 by Jonathan Emmett
Illustrations copyright © 2001 by Vanessa Cabban

You can find out more about Jonathan Emmett's books by visiting his website at www.scribblestreet.co.uk

First U.S. edition 2001

Library of Congress Cataloging-in-Publication Data

Emmett, Jonathan.
Bringing down the moon / written by Jonathan Emmett ; illustrated by Vanessa Cabban. — 1st U.S. ed.
p.   cm.
Summary: Mole is so taken with the beauty of the moon that he
tries to get it from the sky, but eventually learns to appreciate it where it is.
ISBN 0-7636-1577-3
[1. Moon — Fiction. 2. Moles (Animals) — Fiction. 3. Animals — Fiction.] I. Cabban, Vanessa, date, ill. II. Title.
PZ7.E696 Br 2001   [E] — dc21   00-066684

2 4 6 8 10 9 7 5 3 1

Printed in Italy

This book was typeset in Beta Bold. The illustrations were done in watercolor.

Candlewick Press
2067 Massachusetts Avenue
Cambridge, Massachusetts 02140

visit us at www.candlewick.com

Bringing Down the Moon

Jonathan Emmett   illustrated by Vanessa Cabban

CANDLEWICK PRESS
CAMBRIDGE, MASSACHUSETTS

"Hot diggety!" exclaimed Mole
as he burrowed out of the ground
one night. "Whatever's that?"

The moon was hanging in the sky
above him, like a bright silver coin.
Mole thought that it was the
most beautiful thing he
had ever seen.

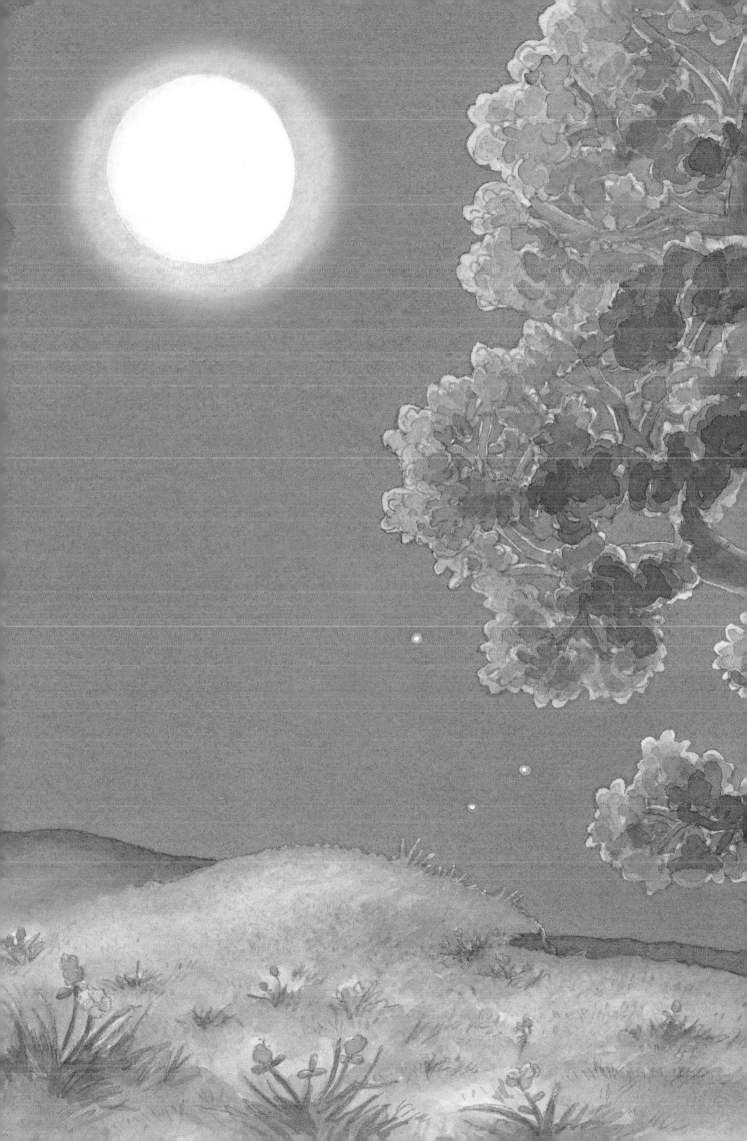

"Whatever it is,
I must have it,"
Mole said to
himself.
"I know. I'll
jump up and
pull it down."

THUMP
THUMP!

THUMPETY

BUMP!

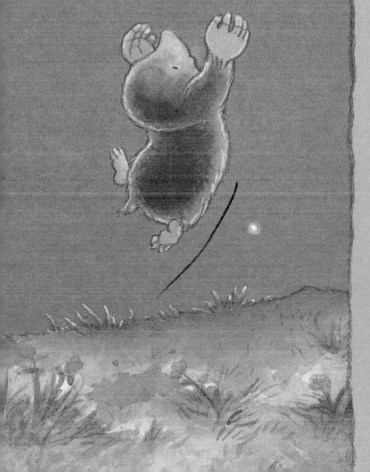

Mole was so busy jumping he didn't think about the noise he was making, and he woke up Rabbit in her burrow.

"Mole!" said Rabbit. "What on earth do you think you're doing?"

"Hello, Rabbit," said Mole. "I'm trying to pull down that shiny thing."

"You mean the moon?" asked Rabbit.

"So that's what it's called," said Mole.

"You'll never do that," said Rabbit. "It's not as close as it looks."

But Mole would
not give up.
"I know," he thought.
"I'll get a stick
and poke it down."
He found a long
stick and poked it
up at the moon.

SWISH
SWISH!

SWISHETY SWISH!

Mole was so busy poking that he tripped over Hedgehog in his bed of leaves.

"Mole," grunted Hedgehog.
"What the weevil are you up to?"

"Hello, Hedgehog," said Mole.
"I'm trying to poke down the moon."

"You'll never do that," said Hedgehog.
"It's not as close as it looks."

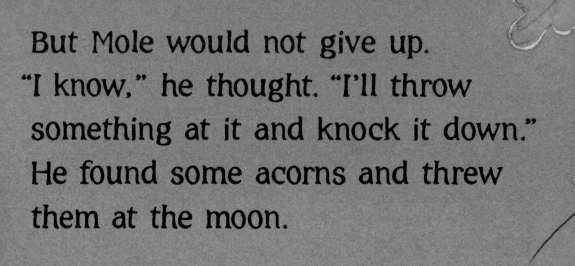

But Mole would not give up.
"I know," he thought. "I'll throw
something at it and knock it down."
He found some acorns and threw
them at the moon.

PLINK PLINK!

PLINKETY PLINK!

"Ouch!"
said Squirrel.
"Mole, have you gone nuts?"

"Hello, Squirrel," said Mole.
"I'm trying to knock down the moon."

"You'll never do that," said Squirrel.
"It's not as close as it looks."

But Mole wanted the moon
so badly, he would not give up.
"I know," he thought. "I'll climb
a tree and carry it down!"

Mole had never climbed a
tree before. It was hard work
and he was scared to be so
far from the ground.
But he kept on going until
he saw the moon
resting in the leaves
above him.

Mole stretched out his paws. But just when he thought he had the moon . . . he slipped!

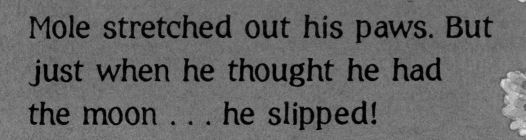

"Oh! Eeek! Ouch! Ooh!"

Mole tumbled down and landed SPLASH!

in the middle of a puddle.

"Hot diggety drat!"
thought Mole. "I almost had it that time."
Then he noticed something
floating in the puddle beside him.
It was pale and wrinkled,
but Mole recognized
it at once.

"The moon," whispered Mole.
"It must have fallen down with me."
He reached out to pick up the moon.
But as soon as he touched it,
it broke into pieces
and vanished.

Mole sat in the puddle and cried.
Rabbit, Hedgehog, and Squirrel
came running up.
"Are you all right, Mole?"
asked Rabbit.

"I'm all right," sobbed Mole.
"But the moon isn't! I pulled it down,
and then I broke it. and it was
SO beautiful . . . and now I'll
never see it again."

"Oh, Mole," said Rabbit,
"you couldn't have pulled down the moon."

"And you couldn't have broken it,"
said Hedgehog.

"And you'll certainly see it again,"
said Squirrel. "Look!"

High up in the sky above them, the moon
was coming out from behind a cloud.

"Oh," whispered Mole, "and it's
just as beautiful as ever."

Mole, Rabbit, Hedgehog, and
Squirrel stood and stared up
at the moon together.

"It is beautiful," said Rabbit.

"Very beautiful!" said Hedgehog.

"Very beautiful indeed!"
said Squirrel.

"Yes,"
said Mole.
"But it's NOT
as close as
it looks!"